WHISPERS IN THE AMAZON

Love's Dance with the Coatimundi

Elena Monteverde

Golden Mirage Publishers

To the captivating and resilient spirit of the Amazon rainforest and its extraordinary inhabitants, especially the Coatimundi, whose unique charm and tenacity have inspired this tale of love. May we always treasure the wonders of the natural world and the magic of unexpected connections.

CONTENTS

Prologue

In the heart of the Amazon rainforest, where the lush foliage kisses the sky and the symphony of the wild resounds, a remarkable love story unfolds. This tale, like no other, is not just about the enchanting Coatimundi, but about the enduring bond that transcends the boundaries of species.

Amidst the emerald canopy and the rhythmic hum of nature's secrets, a scientist and an inquisitive creature find their destinies intertwined. Driven by a shared curiosity about the mysteries of the Amazon, they venture into the depths of the world's largest tropical rainforest, unaware that their paths are about to converge in a way neither could predict.

As the scientist delves into the intricacies of the Coatimundi's life, the charming creature becomes an enigmatic puzzle to be solved. Yet, what begins as a quest for knowledge soon transforms into an exploration of the heart, as the scientist begins to unravel the Coatimundi's mysterious allure.

Through days of relentless exploration and nights filled with the enigmatic beauty of the Amazon, a deep connection forms between them. The scientist learns to see the world through the Coatimundi's eyes, understanding the challenges it faces and the delicate balance it maintains in this untamed realm. In turn, the Coatimundi, too, discovers a kindred spirit in the scientist, someone who shares its curiosity, resilience, and love for the natural world.

Their journey is not just about uncovering the hidden truths of the rainforest; it's about the shared adventure of two souls, from different worlds, who find an inexplicable connection, one that transcends language and understanding. It's a story of patience, trust, and love blossoming in the most unexpected of places.

This love story is a testament to the enduring power of nature to unite even the most unlikely of companions. As they navigate the perils and wonders of the Amazon, their bond deepens, reflecting the intricate ballet of life itself. Their tale is one of companionship, trust, and the unwavering commitment to protect the natural world.

Join us on this captivating journey, as the scientist and the Coatimundi reveal the enchanting secrets of the Amazon, both in the world of science and the world of the heart. Together, they'll leave an indelible mark on the rainforest and each other's lives, forging a love story that transcends boundaries and forever links their destinies to the mysteries of the Amazon.

Chapter 2

Date: January 9, 2023

Dear Diary,

The preceding days have been an unrelenting test of our resolve, as we've valiantly navigated the capricious waters of the Rio Negro, a tributary shrouded in Amazonian mystique and isolation. Confronted by the sheer might of its powerful currents and at the mercy of the fickle moods of nature, we've undertaken an arduous journey through dense, overgrown vegetation that clings to the riverbanks like the emerald tendrils of an ancient forest.

Today, a flicker of jubilation surged through the group, electrifying the air with palpable excitement as we uncovered fresh tracks etched on the mud-laden riverbanks. Dr. Vasquez, with her keen eyes alight with anticipation, knelt down to examine the paw prints, her gloved fingers carefully collecting samples of the earth's signature. She spoke with measured enthusiasm, her words laden with the promise of a significant discovery, rallying us with her unwavering confidence.

As we ventured deeper into this uncharted wilderness, our local guide, Luis, demonstrated his remarkable skills as he effortlessly maneuvered through the tangled undergrowth, a living testament to his people's age-old connection with these lands. His sun-weathered face bore a serene determination, and he guided us with an unparalleled knowledge of the jungle's secrets. His words, spoken in a whisper, were a soothing contrast to the chaos surrounding us, as he shared the tales of Coatimundi's sly elusiveness passed down through generations, further deepening our respect for his wisdom.

Our foray into this terra incognita found us submerged within a labyrinth of verdant chaos. Sarah, our intrepid botanist, her clothing soaked from the incessant rain, bent down to study the intricate plant life that enveloped us. Her love for the jungle's flora shone through, as she marveled at the resiliency of each species, drawing strength from their survival in this harsh environment.

Adding to our tribulations, the heavens were relentless in their offering, gifting us ceaseless rain that blurred the line between the moisture on our brows and the cascading water droplets from the heavens. Yet, amidst the drenched foliage, it was John, our indomitable photographer, who stood out. His camera remained a steadfast companion, capturing the rain-soaked beauty of this otherworldly realm, his artistry undeterred by the inclement weather.

We persevered, soaked to the bone, clinging to the hope that our pursuit of the Coatimundi would soon bear fruit, our enthusiasm undaunted despite the challenges that the rain-soaked Amazon thrust upon our tireless souls. The camaraderie among our group grew stronger with each step, and as we pressed on, we couldn't help but marvel at the fortitude, wisdom, and spirit each member brought to this unforgettable journey. The Amazon had tested us, but we remained resolute, united in our quest for discovery.

Chapter 3

Date: January 15, 2023

Dear Diary,

After an extended period of relentless pursuit, our patience and tenacity finally bore fruit today. The elusive Coatimundi, that cryptic denizen of the Amazonian wilds, revealed itself to us in a breathtaking tableau of the natural world. The profound significance of this moment is etched deep within my soul.

These enigmatic creatures, as we observed today, are beings of social grace and gregarious charm, dwelling in close-knit communities aptly referred to as bands. Dr. Elena Vasquez, our tireless leader and seasoned biologist, exuded an air of sheer joy as we stood witness to this rare spectacle. Her profound understanding of the animal kingdom and the dedication she had poured into this expedition were reflected in her unwavering enthusiasm. She marveled at the Coatimundis, whispering insights to us about their intricate social dynamics, further illuminating her remarkable expertise and passion for these creatures.

As we watched, Sarah, our diligent botanist, leaned in closer, her eyes sparkling with fascination. Her deep love for the Amazon's flora had transcended into an appreciation for the fauna as well. She pointed out how the Coatimundis' presence contributed to the ecosystem's balance, intertwining her passion for botany with the animal world, emphasizing the interconnectedness of all life.

John, our skilled photographer, had his camera poised, ready to capture this ethereal moment. His patience and dedication had been unwavering, and his skill as a visual storyteller had been an invaluable asset to our expedition.

He moved with stealthy grace, aligning his lens to the Coatimundis' ballet-like performance, capturing each delicate motion with an artist's eye.

Luis, our local guide, watched with a contented smile. His connection to this land and its creatures was evident in the way he quietly nodded at the sight. He had brought us here, and the fulfillment of his purpose was written in the lines of his face. His deep respect for the Amazon's secrets had guided us on this journey.

The Coatimundis, with their inquisitive, delicate, and graceful motions, unfolded like a choreographed ballet. Long tails, the quintessential signature of their species,

were held aloft in a proud and assertive manner, while their questing noses delved into the underbrush, seeking the ephemeral treasures of insects and small reptiles that constitute their sustenance.

Their size, somewhat smaller and more agile than my preconceptions had imagined, only served to enhance their ethereal charm. In the verdant embrace of the rainforest, these agile acrobats defied gravity with consummate ease, their tree-climbing skills an astounding spectacle of evolutionary artistry. My camera was poised, capturing this awe-inspiring display, an endeavor I had long prepared for, conscious of the profound contribution it would make to our scientific pursuit. The footage, I am convinced, will prove invaluable, a visual testament to the heart-pounding moments when we were privileged to observe the Coatimundis in their natural habitat.

This encounter is not just a culmination of our relentless efforts, but also a tribute to the boundless wonders of the Amazon, a reminder of the intricate web of life it shelters. In the face of this revelation, I am filled with profound gratitude, for it has unlocked a deeper connection to the natural world and a newfound purpose in our mission. Today, we stood as a team, captivated by the mysteries of the rainforest, celebrating not just the Coatimundi but the unity and dedication that brought us to this awe-inspiring moment.

Chapter 4

Dear Diary,

As the sands of time continue to flow in this verdant haven, our study of the Coatimundis unfolds with ever-deepening fascination. These creatures, once elusive and enigmatic, have unveiled a world of complexity, proving to be far more than mere subjects of scientific curiosity. Their social behavior, intricate as a tapestry, unfurls in captivating detail, revealing a fascinating hierarchy within their bands.

Navigating the labyrinthine depths of this primeval forest has been an enduring test of our resilience. Dr. Elena Vasquez, our unwavering leader, has demonstrated a boundless well of determination and passion for this mission. Her unwavering commitment to understanding these creatures is a testament to her scientific dedication. Her deep, inquisitive eyes, always searching for a new revelation, inspire us all to push forward despite the many challenges.

Sarah, our resident botanist, is a constant source of optimism and wonder. Her gentle enthusiasm for the Amazon's flora and fauna is infectious, and it has added an emotional dimension to our study. Her effervescent spirit lifts our team's morale even in the face of torrential downpours and relentless insects. It is a joy to share the enchantment of this rainforest with her.

Yet, in the midst of this awe-inspiring journey, I've found myself drawn to a kindred spirit. John, our talented photographer, is a fellow explorer who shares my fascination with the Coatimundis. His artistic eye is always keen to capture the intricate details of their behavior. We've spent countless hours in quiet camaraderie, working together to document the fascinating rituals of these creatures. Our conversations have ranged from the scientific to the philosophical, and our bond has grown stronger with each shared experience.

Over the past weeks, as we ventured deeper into the heart of the Amazon, John and I have developed a growing friendship. His laughter, like the chittering of Coatimundis in play, is a comforting soundtrack to our daily pursuits. We've discovered shared dreams and aspirations beyond this expedition, creating a connection that transcends the rainforest and our professional roles. I find myself drawn to his warmth and the genuine interest he shows in every facet of our journey.

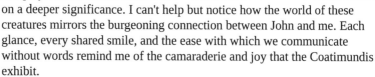

The Coatimundis' grooming rituals and playful interactions have taken on a deeper significance. I can't help but notice how the world of these creatures mirrors the burgeoning connection between John and me. Each glance, every shared smile, and the ease with which we communicate without words remind me of the camaraderie and joy that the Coatimundis exhibit.

Our journey here, Diary, transcends the realm of scientific documentation. It's a voyage of empathy, a deepening bond with the fragile ecosystems of this vital region, and a tribute to the profound mysteries of nature that continue to captivate and astound. As we delve deeper into the world of the Coatimundis, I can't help but hope that our connection, too, will continue to flourish and evolve, much like the rich tapestry of life in this extraordinary rainforest.

Chapter 5

Date: January 25, 2023

Dear Diary,

The recent days have immersed us in an unrelenting study of the Coatimundi's behavior, a journey that delves deep into the enigmatic facets of their lives. Our latest endeavor has entailed the establishment of camera traps, stealthy sentinels poised to unveil the nocturnal mysteries that these creatures guard so jealously. As the days melt into nights in the heart of the Amazon, we find ourselves submerged in a world shrouded in the inky embrace of darkness, a realm where the sounds of the jungle intertwine, creating a symphony that is equal parts beautiful and eerie.

Dr. Elena Vasquez, unwavering in her determination, has been instrumental in guiding us through the challenges of these night-time vigils. Her vast experience in the field has provided us with insights into the meticulous planning and unwavering patience required to capture the Coatimundis in their nocturnal habitat. Her calm, authoritative presence is a source of comfort in this eerie landscape, and her words of encouragement bolster our spirits as we battle the fatigue of sleepless nights.

Sarah's fascination with the Amazon's flora and fauna has taken on a new dimension during these night vigils. She's been instrumental in identifying the various sounds and helping us distinguish between the calls of different creatures. Her keen ear and natural curiosity have enriched our understanding of the jungle's soundscape. She serves as a living encyclopedia of knowledge, connecting us with the intricate, unseen world that surrounds us.

But it was during one particularly challenging night that I truly understood the power of our bond. As we huddled around a malfunctioning camera

trap, frustration

and fatigue began to weigh heavily on us. The jungle seemed darker, more unforgiving than ever before, and our doubts about our mission's success grew.

John, the photographer, always at ease behind his camera, revealed a new dimension of himself. His resourcefulness and problem-solving skills came to the fore as he tinkered with the camera trap, determined to resolve the technical issue. His quiet confidence, paired with his unwavering commitment to the mission, cast a ray of hope in our darkest moment.

The camera traps, our silent witnesses in this spectral realm, remain poised to capture the Coatimundis in their most intimate moments. We've come to realize that the night unveils a dimension of their existence hitherto concealed from us, painting a richer portrait of their behavior and interaction. Our endeavor to comprehend the nuances of their lives is akin to assembling a jigsaw puzzle in the dark, with each camera trap acting as a beacon of insight into the intricate nocturnal world of these creatures.

The journey, despite the challenges, has proven to be an odyssey of enlightenment, a manifestation of our unyielding quest to peel back the veils that cloak the lives of these Coatimundis. It's a journey that leads us deeper into the heart of the Amazon, closer to the heart of nature itself, and closer to the essence of the wild. Each night spent here brings us a step closer to piecing together a clearer picture of the lives that these creatures lead, and with it, a deeper understanding of the natural world we strive to comprehend. In the face of adversity, our unity and shared commitment have become our most potent tools, revealing a profound bond that connects us to the heart of this captivating, enigmatic world.

Chapter 6

Date: January 30, 2023

Dear Diary,

As our journey through the Amazon's labyrinthine depths unfurls, we find ourselves navigating a challenging chapter. Nature, in all its raw magnificence, is both a wondrous spectacle and a stern taskmaster. Last night, we bore witness to one of its capricious and mischievous aspects as our campsite became the stage for a raid by a horde of howler monkeys. Chaos ensued, leaving behind a trail of disarray, disheveled supplies, and a lesson etched in our hearts about life in this untamed realm.

Dr. Elena Vasquez, the unflinching leader of our expedition, displayed a remarkable calm amidst the chaos. Her experience had taught her to adapt to the whims of nature. She swiftly organized our team to protect our precious scientific equipment while ensuring the safety of all members. Her leadership in the face of adversity was a testament to her unwavering dedication to this mission.

Sarah, the botanist, and John, the photographer, worked tirelessly to secure our campsite and repair the damage caused by the simian intruders. Their unwavering determination in the midst of the turmoil was nothing short of inspiring. It was heartening to see how this shared challenge had deepened our bonds, uniting us in a common purpose.

Yet, beneath the surface of this camaraderie, I found myself wrestling with an inner conflict that I had long sought to avoid. John, the fellow explorer with whom I had shared an evolving connection, had been instrumental in resolving the turmoil that the howler monkeys had caused. His reassuring presence and capable actions had left a lasting impression on me.

the night gave way to dawn, we gathered around the smoldering embers of our campfire. I couldn't help but steal glances at John, who, even in the dim light, exuded a quiet strength and a reassuring aura. We shared a brief moment of unspoken understanding, a shared look that held an undercurrent of something more.

It was then that a pang of realization struck me. Our burgeoning connection, the growing attraction that had drawn us together amidst the challenges of this expedition, was one that seemed impossible to sustain. As much as I longed for a deeper bond with John, the jungles of the Amazon were an unforgiving backdrop, a realm where our emotions, like the campsite, could be torn asunder by the unpredictable forces of nature.

The jungle, we are discovering, is a ceaseless crucible of survival, where every creature, great and small, partakes in an enduring contest to maintain its place in this intricate web of life. We, the interlopers in this ancient domain, are not spared from the relentless trials that nature weaves. Our comforts and routines are constantly juxtaposed with the primal instincts of the wild. Our very presence, with our makeshift camp and gear, is a trespass upon the domain of these creatures, who perceive us not as scientists but as intruders in their sacred abode.

Yet, this experience has illuminated the essence of our mission. In understanding the Coatimundis and their existence, we are peering into a microcosm of this eternal struggle for survival. Our temporary discomfort serves as a poignant reminder of the challenges these creatures face daily. They too must remain vigilant, as their predators, from stealthy jaguars to formidable serpents, lurk in the shadows.

In this jungle, our pursuit transcends the mere documentation of facts and figures. It underscores the delicate balance that sustains life in this Eden of biodiversity. Our research serves as a testament to the fragility and resilience of the intricate ecosystems we seek to comprehend. We must be vigilant, not just for the preservation of our own safety but also for the continuation of our quest to unravel the secrets of the Coatimundis.

This is a journey where the boundaries between observer and observed blur, where the unforgiving wild redefines our limits, and where the spirit of discovery finds itself tested and, in doing so, emerges stronger and more profound. But for me, the conflict of emotions is one that seems insurmountable, a challenge I fear might be as un

predictable and uncontrollable as the wild forces of the Amazon itself.

Chapter 7

Date: February 5, 2023

Dear Diary,

Today has been a day of singular fortune, a shimmering gem amidst the unfolding pages of our Amazonian adventure. Our relentless pursuit of the elusive Coatimundis bore fruit anew, and in doing so, etched indelible images into the annals of our memory.

Dr. Elena Vasquez, the unwavering leader of our scientific team, guided us through the tangled labyrinth of the jungle with a sense of purpose that never wavered. Her boundless expertise and deep respect for the Amazon were evident in her every word and action. She approached this newfound success with the same unwavering dedication that had characterized her throughout our expedition.

Sarah, our dedicated botanist, was equally enthralled by the exquisite spectacle of the Coatimundis' acrobatic prowess. Her appreciation for the Amazon's flora had in

stilled a reverence for its creatures, making her an ardent observer of the ecological intricacies that bound this unique environment.

Amidst the awe-inspiring performance of the Coatimundis, I found myself sharing a moment with John, the talented photographer. We marveled at the remarkable footage we were capturing, our shared enthusiasm serving as a silent bond that transcended words. His eyes, like mine, were alight with wonder, and as we worked side by side, the connection that had developed over the course of our journey felt deeper and more profound.

However, amidst the splendor of this revelation, a small disagreement cast a fleeting shadow on our day. While reviewing the footage, John and I

couldn't help but disagree on the narrative that the images painted. He believed that the acrobatic abilities of the Coatimundis were primarily adaptations for efficient foraging, while I was convinced that these skills were also integral to their social structure, enabling playful interactions and strengthening their bonds.

Our argument was a small one, rooted in differing scientific perspectives, but it revealed a deeper layer of our connection. In the heat of the moment, as we passionately defended our viewpoints, the emotional undercurrents surfaced. Our voices may have been raised in disagreement, but our eyes betrayed the unspoken emotions that we had harbored.

Yet, circumstances conspired to keep our true feelings at bay. The jungle, with its ceaseless sounds and captivating distractions, demanded our immediate attention. The disagreement, though significant in the moment, was quickly pushed to the periphery as we returned to the demanding work of documenting the Coatimundis.

As the day melted into the velvety embrace of the Amazonian night, the echoes of our disagreement lingered in the humid air. Our connection, forged through shared experiences and mutual passion, was strengthened by this momentary conflict, but I couldn't help but wonder if it was a sign of the complexities that lie ahead. In the heart of the Amazon, where every day is a test of resilience, both within ourselves and in our connections, we're left with emotions unspoken, bound by circumstance, and tested by the unpredictability of the wild.

Chapter 8

Date: February 10, 2023

Dear Diary,

In the heart of the Amazon, our mission has evolved far beyond the mere act of observation. We've ventured into the realm of understanding, one that carries the weighty mantle of responsibility and stewardship. Our journey, now infused with deeper purpose, transcends the boundaries of our scientific ambitions and takes root in the sacred soil of conservation.

Dr. Elena Vasquez, the unwavering and unyielding leader of our team, has been a beacon of inspiration as we delve deeper into the significance of our research. Her unwavering commitment to understanding the Coatimundis, rooted in a profound love for the Amazon, has become a guiding light for us all. Her leadership transcends the boundaries of science and delves into the realm of environmental advocacy, reminding us of the urgency of our work.

Sarah, the botanist, with her deep appreciation for the Amazon's diverse flora, has become a guardian of the forest's secrets. Her understanding of the intricate relationships between the plants and the Coatimundis has added a layer of depth to our research. She walks through the Amazon with a sense of reverence, as if every step is a step in the pages of a sacred book.

As for John, the photographer, our connection has grown deeper and more profound. We've become not just colleagues but partners in this quest, and the unspoken emotions that simmered beneath the surface have only intensified. His unwavering support and shared dedication have become pillars of strength, an anchor in the tumultuous waters of the Amazon.

But it was during one particularly perilous situation that John and I truly recognized the strength of our bond. While documenting the Coatimundis, we found ourselves in close proximity to a large and agitated jaguar, a creature that embodied both the breathtaking beauty and ruthless danger of the Amazon. The jaguar's predatory intent was palpable, and our hearts raced in the face of this imminent threat.

In that heart-pounding moment, John and I locked eyes, and without words, we understood the gravity of our situation. Fear and adrenaline coursed through our veins, but so did an unspoken determination to survive. We knew that our actions had consequences far beyond ourselves, that the preservation of the Coatimundis and the intricate Amazonian ecosystem depended on our escape.

We slowly and silently retreated, moving in tandem with the grace of Coatimundis themselves. John's hand reached for mine, and our fingers interlocked, a bond forming in that moment of peril. Every rustle of leaves, every breath of the jaguar became a symphony of potential disaster, and yet, we pressed on, our bond and our shared commitment giving us the strength to continue.

The jaguar eventually lost interest, and we were left trembling but unharmed. As we sat in the safety of our camp later that night, our emotions raw, we looked at each other, and in that gaze, we knew. We knew that our connection was forged in the crucible of danger, that it was more profound than words could ever convey.

Our research, therefore, is a voyage of responsibility, a sacred duty that extends beyond science to the very soul of preservation. It's a testament to the profound connection between understanding and conserving. We've become custodians of the Amazon, protectors of an intricate web of existence that extends far beyond the Coatimundis themselves. Our work has evolved into a clarion call, reminding us that the preservation of this environment is not a mere choice but an imperative, a linchpin in the survival of countless species, a pledge to safeguard the soul of the Amazon. And in the face of that jaguar, we not only survived the danger but also recognized the depth of our connection and our shared commitment to protect this breathtaking realm, no matter the risks we face.

Chapter 9

Date: February 15, 2023

Dear Diary,

In the heart of this wild Amazonian tapestry, time unfurls its wings with relentless haste. The days pass like fleeting dreams, each sunrise and sunset echoing the urgency of our quest, for we find ourselves engaged in a race against the inexorable march of time. In our relentless pursuit of knowledge about the enigmatic Coatimundis, it becomes starkly evident that the chalice of comprehension is yet far from brimming, the tapestry of their lives far from complete.

Dr. Elena Vasquez, our fearless leader, continues to be a beacon of inspiration, her unwavering determination guiding us through this intricate journey. Her unwavering commitment to preserving the Amazon is infectious, permeating every aspect of our expedition. Her leadership is a reminder that knowledge and conservation are intrinsically linked, and it's not enough to uncover the secrets of the Coatimundis; we must also protect the habitat they call home.

Sarah, the botanist, has become more than a colleague; she's a guardian of the rainforest's secrets. Her expertise in the intricate relationships between the plants and the animals is a testament to her deep respect for this environment. Her enthusiasm is infectious, reminding us of the interconnectedness of all life here.

And then, there's John, the fellow explorer with whom I've shared more than scientific endeavors. The bond between us has grown deeper with each passing day, and amidst the tapestry of our shared experiences, our connection has become undeniable. We've been through moments of peril and triumph together, and it's clear that our shared passion for the Amazon has given birth to something profound.

It was during one evening, as we sat by the campfire, the flickering flames casting playful shadows on our faces, that our feelings became too powerful to deny. The jungle around us echoed with the chirping of insects and the haunting calls of unseen creatures. The symphony of life in the Amazon served as a backdrop to our unspoken emotions.

John reached for my hand, his fingers interlacing with mine, and his eyes held a depth of emotion that needed no words. As the firelight danced in his eyes, I knew that the connection between us was no longer just about shared experiences; it was about love.

I took a deep breath, feeling the weight of the Amazonian night around us, and I finally said it: "John, I love you."

His eyes lit up with a mixture of surprise and joy, and he whispered, "I love you too." The words, so simple yet profound, hung in the air like a promise. In that moment, amidst the beauty and danger of the Amazon, our connection was no longer just about survival and research; it was about love and a shared commitment to protect this extraordinary realm. The urgency of our quest and the beauty of our love became intertwined, and I knew that together, we were ready to face whatever challenges the Amazon had in store for us.

Chapter 10

Date: February 20, 2023

Dear Diary,

Today, the unyielding jungle delivered a harsh reminder of its relentless nature. In the heart of our relentless quest, a formidable challenge emerged in the form of a major setback. The formidable adversary, invisible and indiscriminate, claimed one of our own, Maria, our lead botanist and a lynchpin in our scientific endeavor.

The culprit? Contaminated water, a treacherous serpent lurking in the river's shadow, unseen and insidious. In the embrace of the jungle, even the most seasoned can fall prey to its capriciousness. We discovered Maria, a paragon of resilience and expertise, laid low by the uncompromising forces of nature. Her illness, like an unexpected tempest, has cast a pall over our once-unwavering determination.

Our medic, Jorge, a dedicated soul who stands as a beacon of hope in these trying times, now tirelessly tends to Maria, endeavoring to pull her back from the brink of this unrelenting malady. With boundless care and the tenacity of a true hero, he strives to mend the breach and restore her to her former self.

Yet, this circumstance presents us with an agonizing crossroads, a dilemma that pierces the very soul of our expedition. To continue without Maria, the guardian of our botanical wisdom, risks both the quality and depth of our research. Her irreplaceable knowledge, her years of experience, they are linchpins upon which the success of our mission precariously balances.

On the other hand, to wait until she is fully restored carries its own set of uncertainties. The jungle is an unforgiving master, and time, like a fickle mistress, marches inexorably onward. To pause our expedition, to shelve our relentless quest for knowledge, is to risk forfeiting the very secrets we have journeyed so far to unlock.

This is the crucible in which our commitment to understanding and preservation is tested. It is a heart-wrenching choice, a moment that compels us to weigh the value of knowledge against the sanctity of a life's well-being. Each passing minute underscores the gravity of our decision, the stakes higher than ever before, as the jungle watches, unforgiving yet beguiling, ever the enigmatic guardian of its secrets.

Amidst this turmoil, John and I have found solace in each other's arms. Our love has become a refuge, a sanctuary of warmth in the midst of uncertainty. As we sit together, gazing at the stars through the dense canopy, our love deepens. We have chosen to stand together, to support one another in this trying time.

And it was under the starlit sky that I found the courage to speak my heart. I turned to John, my heart full of love and uncertainty, and I said, "John, our love has grown amidst the challenges of this journey. I want you to know how much you mean to me. I love you, and I want to face whatever the jungle throws at us together."

He looked into my eyes, a glimmer of emotion dancing in his, and replied, "I love you too. You're my anchor in this storm, and I want to face it all with you." Our words hung in the air like the fragrance of rain on a parched earth, a testament to the strength of our love.

In the midst of uncertainty, our love has become a beacon of hope, a testament to the power of human connection, and a reminder that even in the darkest of times, there can be moments of light and love. We are determined to navigate this crisis as a united front, armed with love and dedication to protect both Maria's well-being and the Amazon's secrets, for these are the twin callings that bind us together.

Chapter 11

Date: February 25, 2023

Dear Diary,

In the heart of the unforgiving Amazon, the weight of a profound decision presses down upon us. The journey that has been a relentless chase through the heart of the jungle is now brought to an abrupt halt, a decision made from the depths of both necessity and prudence. The custodian of our botanical wisdom, Maria, lies in the grip of an insidious illness, and it is her expertise we cannot afford to lose.

The jungle, we have come to understand, is a merciless, labyrinthine enigma, where every step is a potential foray into the unknown. The complexity of this ecosystem, its intricate interactions and delicate balance, requires not just tenacity but a meticulous comprehension of every nuance, and this is what Maria brings to our endeavor. Her knowledge is the rudder steering us through the treacherous waters of discovery, and we cannot afford errors in these uncharted territories.

Hence, with heavy hearts and a profound sense of responsibility, we've taken the decision to pause our relentless journey. Our very mission, now more than ever, becomes a manifestation of the respect and reverence we hold for the jungle's unpredictable and formidable nature. This hiatus is not a capitulation but a strategic maneuver, a testament to our unwavering commitment to the cause of understanding and preservation. It's a recognition that, in the jungle, wisdom and expertise are our greatest allies.

In this unforeseen intermission, we find ourselves drawn into a meticulous review of our findings. The data we've gathered, the footage we've amassed, all undergo a comprehensive scrutiny, an opportunity to uncover insights and patterns that may have eluded us in the headlong rush of the expedition. It is a reflective pause, where the hectic pursuits of exploration make way for contemplation and deeper understanding.

While Maria convalesces under Jorge's care, we seize this hiatus as an opportunity to replenish our supplies, the lifeblood of our journey. Each provision, every ounce of rations, equipment, and communication devices, is meticulously accounted for, a testament to the unforgiving environment that surrounds us.

This, Diary, is a chapter in the tale of our expedition that lays bare the essence of our mission. It is a journey that transcends the confines of simple observation; it is a solemn pledge to the cause of preservation. Every step we take, even those that lead us to pause and reflect, is a testament to the reverence we hold for the jungle's secrets, and to our unwavering determination to honor and protect them.

In the midst of our preparations, John and I find ourselves alone amidst the verdant tapestry of the Amazon. Our love, once a sanctuary in the tumult of our mission, is now a refuge from the uncertainty that shrouds our journey. We find moments of solace in each other's arms, our love deeper than ever.

As we stand near the river's edge, the sun casting a warm, golden glow upon the rippling water, I take John's hand in mine. His eyes, the color of the jungle foliage, meet mine with a depth of affection that warms my heart. I tell him, "John, even in the midst of uncertainty, I've never been so sure of anything in my life. I love you, and I cherish every moment we spend together."

He smiles, his touch gentle and reassuring, and replies, "I love you too. Our love is a beacon in the dark, a reminder that even amidst the challenges, we can find happiness. We'll navigate this together, and I promise to stand by your side through it all."

In that moment, the jungle's cacophony of sounds and the ever-present specter of uncertainty fade into the background. It is just the two of us, wrapped in love's embrace, a sanctuary that nothing can disrupt. Our love is a testament to the power of human connection, a force that can withstand even the harshest of challenges.

As the sun sets over the Amazon, painting the sky with hues of orange and pink, we share a tender kiss, a symbol of our love's enduring strength. It is a moment of bliss amidst the unpredictability of our journey, a reminder

that, even in the heart of the jungle, love can bloom and thrive.

Chapter 12

Date: February 25, 2023

Dear Diary,

After an interlude marked by trepidation and uncertainty, there's a glimmer of hope breaking through the dense Amazonian canopy. Our stalwart botanist, Maria, who had once been felled by the vagaries of the jungle, is now displaying signs of resurgent strength. Her convalescence is a testament to both the human spirit and the healing touch of Jorge, our unwavering medic.

In this temporary hiatus, as Maria finds herself on the path to recovery, a semblance of mirth and positivity has permeated our camp. The camaraderie that had been tested by adversity is now rekindled, as we rally around the resurgence of our dear colleague. Maria, with her boundless botanical wisdom, had long been the bedrock of our scientific exploration. Her expertise and guidance had illuminated the path we trod, a path strewn with leaves and secrets, thorns and revelations. Her return to

health is, for all of us, a symbol of hope and a testament to the indomitable spirit that binds our team.

In this unexpected pause, where our progress was interrupted, we've stumbled upon a different form of bounty. We've donned the mantle of explorers in a broader sense, as we've meandered through the Amazon's untamed tapestry, and stumbled upon hidden gems that weren't originally part of our scientific pursuit. The living treasure trove of biodiversity that this ecosystem cradles has beckoned us with its opulence.

Plant and animal species, hitherto uncharted by our scientific endeavors, have graced us with their presence. Our notebooks and cameras are now filled with documentation of flora and fauna that extend beyond our original

scope. The Amazon, in all its opulent splendor, has revealed its bounty, and we are humbled by the endless diversity that thrives here.

This pause, this intermission that the Amazon herself has gifted us, allows us to marvel at the intricate connections that intertwine our fate with this irreplaceable ecosystem. We are not mere observers; we are integral participants in this delicate dance. The myriad species, from the tiniest insects to the towering trees, each plays a role, and each thread in this ecological tapestry is interconnected.

In these moments of reflection, our expedition finds its deeper meaning. It is a voyage of understanding and preservation, an odyssey that teaches us the interdependence of all life. The Amazon, through the unexpected bounty it bestows upon us during Maria's recovery, reminds us of our role as custodians, protectors, and ambassadors for the intricate and fragile tapestry of existence that it hosts.

As Maria's strength returns, so too does our determination. The jungle, with its timeless wisdom, beckons us forward with a newfound sense of purpose. We will proceed, not just as scientists but as guardians of this irreplaceable ecosystem, and as witnesses to the myriad marvels it has revealed during our unexpected respite.

During this break, John and I have found moments of seclusion under the towering canopy, allowing our love to flourish amidst the green embrace of the Amazon. The tranquility of the jungle and the sense of shared purpose have deepened our connection.

One evening, as the twilight painted the forest in shades of amethyst, we sat on the riverbank, watching the waters flow with silent determination. It was there, amidst the symphony of nature, that we began to discuss our future, to contemplate the path our love would take.

I turned to John, his eyes reflecting the warm hues of the setting sun, and said, "We've faced challenges together, and now we must consider the future. Our love is a treasure amidst this wilderness, and I refuse to let the jungle's trials keep us apart."

He smiled, his hand finding mine, and replied, "I feel the same way. Our love is a source of strength, and it's worth every obstacle we encounter. Let's work together, find a way to make this work, to balance our scientific mission and our love."

And so, in the heart of the Amazon, we began to shape a plan, to find a way to balance our scientific pursuit with our blossoming love. It won't be without its challenges, but as we've learned from the jungle itself, it's the interdependence and adaptation that sustains life. Our love, like the intricate web of existence in the Amazon, can thrive amidst complexity and uncertainty.

Chapter 13

Date: March 5, 2023

Dear Diary,

Today, an unspoken sense of triumph and anticipation lingered in the air, as we resumed our unrelenting quest for the elusive Coatimundi. Our temporary camp, sheltered beneath the verdant canopy of the Amazon, had served as both sanctuary and prison during Maria's recovery. The revival of our lead botanist's health has now spurred us forward, casting aside the heavy weight of uncertainty.

As the sun painted the sky with hues that seemed straight out of a painter's dream, our group prepared to embark. Maria, our guardian of botanical wisdom, showed remarkable improvement. Her resilience and recovery are a testament to the strength that courses through her veins. In her eyes, there is a spark of renewed determination, and it was with a heavy yet hopeful heart that we left behind our makeshift haven to continue our quest.

With Maria back among us, our spirits are revitalized, our resolve unwavering. Her expertise is invaluable, her presence, a lighthouse guiding our scientific journey through the uncharted territories of the Amazon. Her return is a reaffirmation of the unity and purpose that define our team.

As we depart from the safety of our temporary camp, there is an unspoken agreement among us that the challenges that lie ahead, while daunting, will be met with even greater determination. The Coatimundi, an enigmatic creature of the rainforest, is our quarry. With Maria's guidance, we feel better equipped to decipher its mysteries.

In this ceaseless journey, the Amazon unveils its secrets reluctantly, each revelation a testament to the unfathomable depth of this enigmatic realm. We seek not just a fleeting encounter with the Coatimundi but an intimate understanding of its existence, of the intricate interplay between this creature and the vibrant ecosystem that cradles it.

The Amazon, in all its impenetrable majesty, beckons us to uncover its hidden gems. Our pursuit is not merely an endeavor to capture images of a mysterious creature, but a pledge to protect and preserve the intricate tapestry of existence that envelops it.

The resumption of our expedition is a return to the core of our mission— a journey of understanding, discovery, and conservation. With Maria back on board, we venture forth with renewed vigor and a sense of purpose that transcends the challenges we face.

This, dear diary, is not just a continuation but a reinvigoration of our relentless pursuit. It is a reaffirmation of our commitment to knowledge, preservation, and, most importantly, to the secrets of the Amazon that await our discovery.

In the heart of the jungle, where our love had found a moment of respite amidst the relentless pursuit of our scientific mission, a shadow looms. It is an entity, an unknown force, that seeks to separate John and me, to cast a veil of uncertainty over our blossoming relationship. This force, shrouded in mystery, has disrupted our harmonious existence.

One evening, as John and I sat by the firelight, sharing stories of our past and dreams of our future, an eerie presence descended upon our camp. The nocturnal symphony of the Amazon ceased abruptly, and an eerie stillness hung in the air. The unspoken tension between us was palpable.

Without warning, a cacophony of animal calls erupted around us, as if the very creatures of the jungle were in a frenzy. It was a disturbance that defied explanation, an intrusion that rattled our core. In that moment, I turned to John, my eyes reflecting the unease that gripped my heart.

"John," I whispered, "something is amiss. The jungle seems to warn us, as though it knows of a threat."

He nodded, his grip on my hand firm, and replied, "I sense it too. But no matter what force seeks to separate

us, we must stand strong. Our love is a force of nature in its own right, and we'll overcome whatever challenges come our way."

As the night wore on, we found solace in each other's arms, determined not to let this mysterious force cast a shadow on our love. We would face this enigmatic adversary together, for our love had become an unyielding bond amidst the challenges of the Amazon.

In the heart of this untamed wilderness, where nature herself seems to conspire against us, our love has become a sanctuary. We stand united, unyielding, and resolute, ready to face whatever forces threaten to separate us.

Chapter 14

Date: March 10, 2023

Dear Diary,

With each passing day in the heart of the Amazon rainforest, our expedition has transformed into an odyssey of wonder and discovery. The depths of this emerald realm, with its hidden treasures and enigmatic creatures, continue to astound us. Our relentless pursuit of the Coatimundi has led us deeper into this wilderness, where the breathtaking biodiversity of the Amazon has unveiled itself in all its glory.

As we venture into the labyrinthine depths of the rainforest, we are greeted by an ever-shifting kaleidoscope of life. The Amazon's biodiversity is a testament to nature's ingenuity. Each dawn heralds new revelations, new species that grace our path with their existence. The enchanting melodies of exotic birds, the fleeting glimpse of vibrantly colored butterflies, and the haunting calls of unseen creatures are a daily symphony that fills the air.

Our primary objective remains the Coatimundi, a creature that has eluded our understanding for far too long. Yet, as we traverse this intricate tapestry of life, our documentation of other species has become a mission in itself. The Amazon, it seems, is more than willing to share its secrets. Each new discovery contributes to the wider understanding of this magnificent ecosystem, painting a more comprehensive portrait of its intricacies.

Our notebooks, filled with sketches and observations, are testaments to the variety of life that thrives here. We've marveled at the iridescent plumage of exotic birds, the vibrant diversity of butterflies, and the stealthy grace of jaguars that prowl through the undergrowth. Every encounter is a brushstroke in the painting of the Amazon, an ever-evolving masterpiece that embodies the ceaseless cycle of life and death.

The Amazon's rainforest, with its towering giants and labyrinthine undergrowth, is a living treasure trove of biodiversity. It's a world where the boundaries between species blur, and the interconnectedness of life becomes manifest. This expedition is not just a quest to reveal the Coatimundi's secrets but a pledge to safeguard the entire ecosystem in which it thrives.

With each stride deeper into the Amazon, our spirits remain unwavering. The thrill of discovery, the dance of life that envelops us, fuels our determination. This rainforest is not just a place of beauty but a sanctuary of invaluable knowledge, a treasure chest of life's wonders. Each step forward is a testament to our commitment to understanding, preserving, and cherishing the untamed heart of the Amazon.

As we press on, dear diary, we do so with the knowledge that we are more than mere observers; we are stewards of this irreplaceable wilderness. Our journey continues, driven by an insatiable curiosity and a profound reverence for the majesty of the Amazon and the creatures that call it home.

In the heart of this enchanting rainforest, where our love once thrived amidst the backdrop of nature's grandeur, there is now an insurmountable chasm. It is a divide, an impasse that appears as formidable and impenetrable as the very Amazon itself. Our love, John's and mine, once a vibrant beacon in the midst of this wilderness, now finds itself tested beyond the brink of endurance.

The forces that seek to separate us have grown stronger. They are like the shadows that creep across the forest

floor at dusk, an ominous presence that has lurked on the periphery of our existence. They cast a dark cloud over our relationship, and their purpose remains inscrutable.

In the darkest hours, as we lay together beneath the sprawling canopy, the jungle itself seemed to mirror the somberness that gripped us. The air was heavy with a foreboding silence, as if the very atmosphere sensed our turmoil. John and I, our hands entwined, shared words of anguish and hope, searching for a way to bridge this insurmountable divide.

"Maria," John said, his voice tinged with frustration, "I can't bear to see us torn apart like this. Our love is a force of nature, just like this jungle. It's indomitable, Maria, and no matter the obstacles, we must fight to overcome them."

I nodded, the tears glistening in my eyes, and replied, "John, our love is our greatest strength. But these forces, they are like the relentless currents of the Amazon River, pulling us in different directions. We need to find a way to navigate this perilous course together."

As the night draped its inky veil over the rainforest, we held each other tightly, pledging to confront the shadowy forces that threatened to tear us asunder. The future remained uncertain, but in that moment, our love felt as untamed and as enduring as the very Amazon that enveloped us.

In the heart of the Amazon, where we once found solace and love, we now face the ultimate test. It's a challenge that we are determined to surmount, for our love is a force of nature, resilient and unwavering. In the depths of this enigmatic wilderness, we stand together, ready to confront whatever forces dare to keep us apart.

Chapter 15

Date: March 15, 2023

Dear Diary,

The relentless passage of time within the Amazon is etched on our very beings. As we delve deeper into the rainforest's embrace, the relentless heat and humidity surround us like an oppressive shroud. Each step we take through the dense undergrowth is a testament to the hardships we endure, and yet, every challenge is a small price to pay for the treasure trove of knowledge we are unearthing.

This journey has led us to the discovery of Coatimundi nests high in the treetops. These elevated abodes are a testament to the creatures' arboreal lifestyle, a revelation that has illuminated another facet of their existence. It's a breakthrough that will undoubtedly enhance our understanding of their behavior, habitat, and the intricacies of their lives within this lush sanctuary.

The dense Amazon canopy is a labyrinth of wonders and trials. The seemingly endless days of rain, which blur the boundaries between earth and sky, conspire with the ever-present humidity to create an environment that seems determined to challenge our resolve. It is as if the very elements of the Amazon have conspired to test the limits of our endurance. Our path is not merely marked by footsteps; it's etched with sweat, marked by the countless obstacles we've overcome, and bathed in the ever-present sounds of the jungle.

And yet, with every setback comes a revelation, with every hardship, a reward. We delve deeper into the world of the Coatimundi, uncovering not only the secrets of their behavior but the intricate social tapestry that defines their existence. These remarkable creatures are not merely solitary beings navigating the Amazon; they are the architects of a complex society.

In the shadowed thickets, beneath the towering canopy, we've unveiled their social dynamics and organization, a revelation that challenges our preconceived notions of complexity within the animal kingdom. There's an unspoken hierarchy, a subtle dance of dominance and submission that underpins their daily lives. In the realm of the Coatimundi, a pecking order exists, a mirror to the systems that govern societies of more 'sophisticated' species.

Amidst the relentless challenges posed by the Amazon's relentless rain and tangled underbrush, we've immersed ourselves in patient observation. It's a study that tests our resolve, but in turn, rewards us with ever-deepening understanding. The mysteries of the Coatimundi's existence begin to unfurl, revealing their remarkable bonds, their inquisitiveness, and their foraging skills.

The essence of community is tangible among the Coatimundis, reflected in their grooming rituals, where meticulous care and bonding play out. The tender touches of their paws on one another's fur are a tactile language of unity. Playful interactions mirror the universal spirit of youthful camaraderie, while their keen noses explore every nook and cranny of their verdant home, deciphering the language of the jungle.

The Amazon rainforest serves as the ever-changing backdrop for their graceful maneuvers. Leaping through the canopy, traversing from one branch to another, the Coatimundis reveal their agility, a testament to the demands of survival in this challenging environment. We observe their insatiable curiosity as they explore their world, ever-watchful, and endlessly inquisitive.

Our meticulous data collection has also laid bare the versatility of their diet. The Coatimundis are opportunistic omnivores, making the most of the Amazon's bounty. Their foraging takes them from the luscious sweetness of ripe fruits to the crispy delights of insects, and even to the capture of small rodents. Their adaptability in the face of nature's diverse menu is a reflection of the wild's enduring resourcefulness.

With every day that passes in the heart of the Amazon, our understanding grows deeper, our connection to the Coatimundi more profound. Our journey is one of revelation, a humble attempt to decipher not only the lives of these captivating creatures but the intricate dance of the entire ecosystem that surrounds them.

As we continue our arduous trek, dear diary, we are propelled by a relentless quest for knowledge. The Amazon remains an eternal enigma, and every step forward reaffirms our commitment to unveiling the secrets of the Coatimundi and, in doing so, to honor the mysteries of the world's most magnificent rainforest.

In the midst of this awe-inspiring journey of discovery, amidst the trials and triumphs of the Amazon, John and I stand side by side. Our love, once threatened by the forces of the jungle and the enigmatic shadows that sought to tear us apart, has emerged even stronger and more resolute. The jungle, like our love, is a place of beauty, wonder, and relentless challenges.

The same resilience we see in the Coatimundis, the unity in their social bonds, and the determination they exhibit in the face of adversity have become our inspiration. The challenges that once threatened to extinguish our love have now become the crucible in which its strength is forged.

"Maria," John said one evening, his eyes reflecting the fire of determination, "we've faced down the forces that tried to keep us apart.

Like these Coatimundis, we've exhibited the same tenacity and strength in adversity."

I nodded, my heart brimming with love and conviction. "John, our love is a force of nature, and we will not be deterred by the jungle's tests. We are together, and together, we will overcome anything that dares to challenge us."

In the heart of the Amazon, where we confront the boundless mysteries of the jungle and the intricate tapestry of the Coatimundis' existence, we have made a choice. We have chosen each other, and in that choice, we've committed to face down any force that dares to separate us. Our love, like the Amazon, is relentless, beautiful, and enduring.

Our journey through the heart of this extraordinary wilderness is not just an exploration of nature's wonders but a testament to the power of love in the face of adversity. Together, we are unbreakable, and together, we will unravel the secrets of the Amazon and, in the process, our love story will become an indelible part of its legacy.

Chapter 16

Date: March 20, 2023

Dear Diary,

Our relentless pursuit of the Coatimundi in the Amazon, like the river itself, has encountered turbulence, yet we press on, unwavering in our quest. The challenges have multiplied; heavy rains, swollen rivers, and nature's fury are testing our resolve. Our equipment bears the scars of our battles with the elements, and our progress has been slowed. But the jungle remains unrelenting, and we, in turn, remain vigilant and resourceful.

As we journey deeper into the heart of this unforgiving wilderness, the Amazon's elements conspire to challenge our very essence. The heavy rains have cast the river into a furious torrent, its waters surging with the reckless abandon of nature. Navigating these treacherous currents tests the mettle of even the most seasoned of explorers. Our equipment, the tools of our trade, have suffered under the relentless assault of rain and mud. They bear the dents and scars of our struggles, a testament to the battles we've waged.

The rainforest's grip upon us is unyielding, and every step through its dense undergrowth is an arduous journey through twisted vines and thorny thickets. The Amazon's humidity hangs like a heavy cloak, drenching us in sweat and testing our endurance with every stride. The jungle's omnipresent cacophony, from the calls of unseen creatures to the whispering leaves, is a symphony of chaos and life. It reverberates through our very souls.

In the face of these challenges, the indomitable spirit of the Amazon and its elusive inhabitants only heightens our determination. We are cast as humble players in a grand theatre of discovery, battling against the relentless forces of nature in our pursuit of understanding.

Yours, in the relentless pursuit of knowledge amidst the forces of nature.

Chapter 17

Date: March 25, 2023

Dear Diary,

Our relentless pursuit of the Coatimundi in the Amazon's depths has once again brought us to a thrilling and illuminating encounter. As we tracked a group through the dense jungle, we were privileged to witness a mesmerizing and unusual interaction between the Coatimundis and a large snake. The moment was a testament to both the resilient survival strategies of the Coatimundi and the intricate tapestry of life in this primal wilderness.

Our excursion led us to a group of Coatimundis nestled amidst the thick vegetation. It was during this silent observation that the jungle unveiled an extraordinary spectacle before our eyes. A large snake, its sinuous form gliding stealthily through the undergrowth, approached the Coatimundis' sanctuary. It was a serpentine predator, coiled in silent threat, its intentions shrouded in the enigma of its species.

In that critical moment, the Coatimundis revealed their astonishing collective defense strategy. In unison, they formed a protective circle around their young, creating a living shield of furry bodies. Their tails rose like sentinel flags, their eyes locked on the intruder. But what left us in awe was their collective chorus of high-pitched calls, a symphony of unity that resonated through the jungle.

The Coatimundis' tactics seemed to unsettle the snake, for it hesitated in the face of this vibrant, vocal barrier. The confrontation was a testament to the Coatimundis' social bonds, their capacity for collective action, and their willingness to protect their offspring at any cost.

In the end, the snake, outmatched by the determination of the Coatimundis, chose to retreat, slithering away into the shadows. As it departed, we were left to marvel at the dynamic display of the Coatimundi's collective defense strategy. It was a moment that revealed the depths of their social bonds, their intelligence, and their formidable adaptability in this realm of predators and prey.

As we watched the Coatimundis protect their young, it was impossible not to see a parallel in our own journey through the Amazon. Our commitment to understanding these creatures and their environment is a testament to our enduring spirit and the lengths to which we are willing to go for the cause of knowledge. Just as the Coatimundis united to shield their young, we, too, have united to protect our scientific mission.

Yours, in awe of the Amazon's wonders and the unwavering spirit of its inhabitants.

Chapter 18

Date: March 30, 2023

Dear Diary,

Our epic journey through the heart of the Amazon is drawing to a close. We stand on the precipice of returning to the scientific community with a treasure trove of data and footage on the Coatimundi, and our hearts brim with excitement. The Amazon, with all its wild, wondrous glory, has left an indelible mark on our souls, imprinting a place of unparalleled beauty and complexity.

As I reflect on our journey, I'm struck by the resonance between the remarkable creatures we've studied and our own resilience in the face of adversity. The Coatimundis, these agile acrobats of the jungle canopy, have shown us the beauty of adaptability and the art of thriving in their challenging environment.

Much like the Coatimundis who dance through the treetops with grace, navigating a world that challenges even the most nimble of creatures, we, too, have shown our ability to rise above obstacles. The dense underbrush of challenges, the towering canopy of setbacks, and the unpredictability of the jungle's nature may have tested our resolve, but it has also brought out the strength of our spirit.

In the face of harsh conditions, we've remained undaunted, learning to adapt and thrive. Just as the Coatimundis use their long tails for balance, we've found equilibrium through teamwork and perseverance. We've reached for new heights of understanding, much like the Coatimundis reach for fruits in the upper canopy, never allowing the complexity of our environment to deter us.

Through it all, we've discovered the beauty of our shared journey, a journey that has led us to a profound connec

tion with the natural world. Much like the Coatimundis protect their young, forming a living shield against threats, we've protected our mission, cherishing our pursuit of knowledge. We, too, have unveiled our ability to adapt, survive, and thrive.

In the Amazon, where every creature, large or small, finds its own path to survival, we have unearthed not only the secrets of the Coatimundi but also the enduring human spirit. Our expedition, in all its complexities, has revealed the intricate web of life that sustains this rainforest.

Now, on the cusp of our journey's end, I find myself grateful for the Amazon's lessons, the Coatimundi's graceful resilience, and the strength that the pursuit of knowledge has bestowed upon us. The time has come to weave together the stories of the jungle, to encapsulate the symphony of life, and to return to the world we left behind, forever changed by the wild, wondrous heart of the Amazon.

Yours, forever touched by the spirit of the jungle.

Chapter 19

Date: April 5, 2023

Dear Diary,

Our momentous journey through the depths of the Amazon is nearing its conclusion. It's a time of profound reflection and a deep sense of gratitude. Our quest, initially to discover the Coatimundi, has revealed far more than a singular species; it has unveiled an entire ecosystem, a remarkable tapestry of life that is the Amazon. As we prepare to depart, we find ourselves humbled by this awe-inspiring experience, profoundly aware of the vital importance of preserving this unique environment for the generations that will follow.

In the face of this profound journey, a chapter of our lives is coming to a close, but the lessons we've learned and the experiences we've gathered will forever remain etched in our hearts and minds. It's with a sense of fulfillment that we contemplate the impact we've had on our understanding of the Amazon and the creatures that inhabit it.

We've witnessed the Coatimundis' intricate social structures, marveled at their acrobatic feats amidst the canopy, and delved into their roles as ecological keystones. Our pursuit of knowledge has not only enriched our scientific understanding but has also ignited within us a profound commitment to conservation.

The Amazon, draped in its astonishing biodiversity, has whispered secrets of survival, balance, and resilience. It has revealed the intricate dance between nature's wonders and the importance of safeguarding it for the future. Just as the Coatimundis disperse seeds that ensure the growth of the forest, we feel the seeds of inspiration planted deep within our souls.

Our journey's end also marks the beginning of new goals and aspirations. We've been inspired by the majesty of the Amazon and the importance of its preservation. We've discussed plans to continue our work, both as scientists and as advocates for conservation. We envision ourselves returning to these lush, emerald depths, not as mere observers but as active protectors of this fragile paradise.

As we navigate the labyrinthine waterways that lead us out of the Amazon, our hearts swell with the conviction that this journey is only the beginning of a lifelong commitment. We dream of expanding our research, raising awareness about the Amazon's irreplaceable value, and collaborating with organizations and individuals dedicated to the preservation of this wondrous ecosystem.

With the setting sun casting a golden hue on the river's surface, we speak of educational initiatives, community involvement, and the vital importance of fostering a harmonious coexistence between humans and nature. Our shared vision is to leave behind a legacy of understanding, conservation, and respect for the Amazon, just as the Coatimundis contribute to the forest's regeneration.

The completion of this journey is not an end; it is a milestone, a turning point in our lives. It is a commitment to protect the magnificent tapestry of life we've had the privilege to witness, to preserve the Amazon's essence for generations yet unborn. Our dreams and aspirations, like the countless secrets of the Amazon, remain boundless. With hope in our hearts and purpose in our steps, we move forward, forever united in our dedication to this unparalleled realm of life.

Yours, stepping into the future with a deep sense of purpose.

Chapter 20

Date: April 10, 2023

Dear Diary,

We've returned to our base camp in Manaus, bringing with us a treasure trove of knowledge about the Coatimundi and the Amazon rainforest. Our expedition, filled with challenges and triumphs, stands as a testament to the resilient spirit of exploration and underscores the vital importance of conservation. As I reflect on our journey, I can't help but contemplate the next adventure, another venture into the realms of the unknown, where we'll continue to unveil the secrets of our extraordinary world. This diary, brimming with our experiences and revelations, will serve as a testament to our mission, a testament to our unwavering commitment to understanding and safeguarding the natural wonders of our precious planet.

We've come full circle, returning from the Amazon, not just as explorers but as storytellers of nature's secrets. Our journey was far more than a mission of discovery; it

was an odyssey through the Amazon's heart, a deep dive into the intricate marvels of life, and a testament to the resilience and adaptability of both human and animal.

I think back to those humid, intense days where we followed the trail of the Coatimundi, and I can't help but draw parallels between their tenacity and our own. We pressed on through tangled vines and relentless rain, faced challenges with unwavering resolve, and journeyed into the nocturnal world of the Amazon's denizens with insatiable curiosity. The Coatimundi is not just a species of interest; it is a symbol of our own capacity to persevere in the face of adversity.

The camera traps unveiled the Coatimundi's world after dark, a realm of shadows and mysteries. It echoed our journey, where we navigated the dense forest not just under the canopy of daylight but in the inky embrace of night. We reveled in their agile night-time dances, mirroring our own determination to understand the secrets of this uncharted territory.

Our exploration, I now realize, is not just a scientific endeavor. It is an immersion into the depths of our planet's intricate workings, a journey that teaches us about the importance of balance, resilience, and the intertwined fates of all living creatures. The Amazon, with its relentless beauty and formidable challenges, reminds us that our own existence is closely entwined with the survival of our planet's most precious ecosystems.

As we pack our findings and return to the world we know, our hearts brim with gratitude. The Amazon, with all its breathtaking complexity, is a reminder that we are but passengers on this planet. Our mission extends beyond mere discovery; it is a calling to preserve the fragile beauty of the natural world.

The experience has left a profound mark on my heart, not just as a scientist but as a human being. It has reminded me that the lessons we learn from nature are not confined to data and scientific insights. They are lessons of patience, of resilience, and of our responsibility to safeguard the wonders of the world.

And as the journey unfolds, I look to the horizon with excitement, contemplating what lies ahead. Our exploration is not yet complete; it is a lifelong endeavor. Our love, like the Coatimundis' dance through the treetops, is an intricate ballet of companionship, trust, and shared dreams. Our future, I hope, holds many more chapters of discovery, love, and the unwavering commitment to protect the natural world.

Yours, forever devoted to the mysteries of nature.

Epilogue

Years have passed since that fateful expedition into the heart of the Amazon, where the scientist and the Coatimundi's paths first crossed. Their love story, an extraordinary bond that began amidst the towering trees and echoing calls of the rainforest, continued to flourish in the world beyond the Amazon's embrace.

The scientist, forever devoted to the mysteries of nature, returned to the world with a heart filled with not only newfound knowledge but also a profound appreciation for the intricate workings of the natural world. The experiences shared with the Coatimundi served as a constant reminder of the lessons learned in the depths of the rainforest - lessons of patience, resilience, and the responsibility to protect our planet's fragile ecosystems.

The Coatimundi, too, left an indelible mark on the scientist's heart. As they journeyed back to their human world, the memory of the Coatimundi's inquisitive eyes and agile, nighttime dances continued to dance in the scientist's thoughts. This remarkable creature had revealed not only the secrets of the rainforest but had also opened a gateway to a deeper understanding of the interconnectedness of all living beings.

In the years that followed, the scientist remained a staunch advocate for conservation and the protection of the Amazon. The love story between the scientist and the Coatimundi became a symbol of the intrinsic relationship between humanity and the natural world. Their shared dreams and commitment to safeguarding the wonders of the Earth inspired others to follow in their footsteps.

The Coatimundi continued its life in the depths of the Amazon, thriving in the ever-changing ecosystem. Although the scientist had returned to their own world, their hearts remained forever linked through the unbreakable bond forged during their extraordinary adventure.

As the years rolled on, the scientist never forgot the enchanting creature that had touched their soul. Their love story with the Coatimundi, like the

Amazon itself, was a timeless narrative of enduring connection, teaching the world that love, in all its forms, could bridge the gap between species and kindle a fire that burned brightly, even in the darkest corners of the world.

And so, the scientist's journey of discovery, love, and commitment to nature continued, with the lessons learned from their Amazonian odyssey guiding their path. For they knew that their exploration was not yet complete, and their love, like the Coatimundi's dance through the treetops, was an intricate ballet of companionship, trust, and shared dreams - forever devoted to the mysteries of nature and the timeless love story born in the heart of the Amazon rainforest.

Printed in Great Britain
by Amazon